The Forest

Mustafa Kulle

ISBN paperback: 978-1-910461-38-9
ISBN ebook: 978-1-910461-39-6

ACKNOWLEDGEMENTS

Special Thanks to my Editor Dr. Stephen Carver

Special Thanks to my family and friends for all their love and support.

Mustafa Kulle

Nikolai held his wife close as she wept. They were among all the families who lost their elders the other night; all of whom died at the same time. Hundreds of bodies were laid out in front of them on wooden altars. One by one, each one was lit with a torch. The funeral was held outdoors. The weather was cold with an intermittent breeze. Grey clouds concealed the sky, there was no sunlight in sight. It looked like it was about to rain. The town's cathedral wasn't big enough to house all the mourners. He looked on as the flames penetrated the blackened bodies.

"By the gods, what could have possibly done this?" He whispered to himself.

The town's Priest recited prayers. He took out an incense burner and placed a match inside it. The smoke burst from the container, a sickening stench that made him choke and everyone else around him gag. One person who stood close by vomited.

"Put it out! Put it out!" The Mayor stepped forward. A few others joined in as they assisted in overturning the container, putting out the burning dried leaves with the heels of their boots.

"What did you put in there?" asked the Mayor.
"The same incense I use all the time," the Priest replied.
"Well, next time, check before a funeral," the Mayor commanded.

To that, Nikolai thought to himself; "There won't be any more funerals for quite some time," as he watched.
"I'm hungry," said his daughter, Gretel.
"Me too," his son, Markus, added.
"I know," said their mother, Maria. She stroke the little boys head.
Nikolai placed his hand on his daughter's cheek.

Just then, a Town guard on a horse rode over towards the crowd. He jumped off his horse and ran over to the Mayor. To that, the Mayor turned around and held his arm up.
"Attention everyone. The emergency supplies have arrived. Make your way to the market."

The crowd was quiet. On any other day, the town's people would have rushed over. But their response was slower than usual. Most people wanted to stay a while longer. The flames ahead of them burned their mothers, their fathers, and grandparents.
"There is enough for everyone."

"Come on, let's go to the market, you get some food and I will go to the blacksmith to get my axe sharpened. Then we can go home," said Nikolai. He led the family

Just then, as the crowd slowly dispersed, the town's Physician stepped forward onto the stone platform. He took out a scarf and wrapped it around his head covering his nose and mouth taking extra care not to breathe in any more of the fumes. Then he took out a small teaspoon and a test tube from his long coat. He knelt down, scooped up some the burnt powder on the stone and poured it into his test tube, shaking the teaspoon as he did. The test tube was about a quarter full; that was enough for him. He rose up, sighed, and walked up to the Priest, lowering his scarf from his nose down underneath his chin. He approached the Priest.

"Father," he said.

"You again?!" the Priest raged.

"Father," he said again, "can I have a sample of that incense powder please?"

"No you can't!" the Priest bellowed and walked away.

"Very well, have it your way," he whispered to himself as he walked in the opposite direction.

***

Nikolai entered the Blacksmith's shop.

"Hello Shukri," Nikolai greeted.

"Ahh, Nikolai. Hello, my good friend," Shukri the Blacksmith responded.

"How are things with you?"

"Aye. Very busy these days. I haven't had a moment's rest for a long time now."

"Well, don't work yourself to death. We've had enough deaths already," said Nikolai. "After last night and today, I want things to go back to normal so we can get on with our lives and feed our families."

"Aye," Shukri nodded in agreement.

"Anyway, I need you to sharpen my axe." Nikolai held out his axe, the blade was blunt.

"I'm afraid that will take a while. I already have many axes in order. See?" He pointed to a row of axes at the back of his shop, each one inadequate for its job, with dents, some with cracks, while the rest were blunt.

"You should get another apprentice to work with your son," suggested Nikolai.

"I did. But he didn't show up."

"He didn't want the job?" Nikolai enquired.

"No. He's missing. It was Harold's son. He came to shop the other day and asked me where he was. I told him I didn't know."

"Ran away from home perhaps?" asked Nikolai.

"Who knows?"

"Say, Nikolai, have you ever thought of getting yourself a sharpening stone wheel?" Shukri asked.

"No, it's very expensive," Nikolai answered.

"You've been a regular customer of mine for years. I can get a good one for you at a special price. Leave a deposit today and I can have it brought to you in a week. You can pay the rest later," offered Shukri.

"That's very kind of you," said Nikolai. "I'll think about it. But what's brought this on?"

"You see, there are more wood cutters than ever before;generation after generation of woodcutters.There aren't enough blacksmiths like myself to keep up with it all."

"Makes sense," Nikolai agreed.

"Besides, the kingdom relies on our town for its supply of lumber. Our town keeps expanding, yet there seems to be an endless supply of trees from our forest. Have you never wondered will there be any trees left?"

"I don't think so," Nikolai answered. "As far as I'm concerned, that forest will always be here. It's our livelihood. For hundreds of years our fathers cut trees from that forest. We are wood cutters. There are enough trees to last generations more."

Another woodcutter entered the shop carrying an axe.

"Hello there gents," said the woodcutter.
"Hello, Andreas," Nikolai and Shukri greeted him.
"Say Shukri, will you sharpen my axe?"
"Okay, about that deposit," Nikolai turned to Shukri, "Here's some gold." He took out a small bag of coins and put it on the counter.
"Done," said Shukri.
"Bye," Nikolai said as he left the Blacksmith's shop.

***

The market was busy with people trying to carry on with their lives, but everyone looked sad, and walked in a slower pace. Carts that came from outside the town were loaded with food. Everything else in the town was in limited supply. Town soldiers made sure everyone had a fair share. The stall owners were not calling out their wares. Conversation was minimal. There wasn't much to say, everyone lost their elder relatives at the same time. The sky remained grey but darker than before. They had brought the funeral with them into the town centre.

Maria was in the market with the two children shopping when she encountered some familiar faces.

"Hello Maria," her sister Gloria greeted. "Where's your husband?"

"Hello Gloria, he's gone to the blacksmith," Maria replied.

"How are you feeling after that funeral?"

"Oh, I feel terrible. I still can't understand how all the town's elderly could die so suddenly," she answered.

"Not to mention, the way they died too. They looked like they saw ghosts, they had their eyes wide open, and their gaping mouths looked like they were screaming. And they were cold and stiff."

"Oh God, I'm trying not to think about it," Maria said. "I'll never forget that. It's as if it was some sort of curse."

"Hush!"Gloria grabbed her arm and shook it. "You utter such a thing you will put a curse on us all!"

"Then what would you call this?" Maria asked.
"Just don't say that again," Gloria insisted. She looked around to see if anyone else was listening. Some glanced but looked on ahead, the rest minded their own business.

They waited in a line for quite some time. Markus rolled his eyes and sighed with boredom.
"Mother, how long do we have to keep doing this?"
"For as long as it takes," Maria replied.
"Why don't we go and get our food from somewhere else?"

"Don't be silly, it's too far," said Gretel.
"Then why don't we move?" asked Markus
"The whole kingdom of Konendara depends on Father's lumber," Gretel began. "Where else do you think he gets the money from? Father is a woodcutter. Every day he cuts down trees, and gives the wood to the Mayor in exchange for money. The Mayor then sells the wood to all the other towns that need wood. You know, to build houses and make things like furniture and tools. Grandfather was a woodcutter, his

father was a woodcutter too, and so on. We are a family of woodcutters everyone depends on. You see, none of this would ever be possible without that forest we live nearby. It's so big. After all these generations it never seems to run out of trees."

"I guess so," said Markus, "But why- "

"It's the same reason we are lining up to buy fish. The fish are brought to our town from elsewhere because we don't live near any lakes or by the sea. The same way the woodcutters provide wood for those places, the fishmongers provide us with fish."

"Oh, okay," said Markus. He paused for a moment. "But we used to get our fruit from the forest, so why do we get them from outside now?"

"I don't know. It wasn't always like this. We used to pick blackberries and now they taste horrible, " Gretel answered.

"All the fruit and vegetables have become inedible over the last year," said Gloria. "As soon as you bought them from the market they rot before you brought them home."

Maria leaned towards Gloria and whispered,

"A curse perhaps?"

Gloria elbowed her, "Don't be stupid!" she growled. She looked around in embarrassment. Maria tutted.

"Oh Gloria, why are you being so serious?"

"Look, I don't want God to punish us anymore. Things are bad enough as it is. So don't make it worse!" she whispered through her teeth.

"Punish? Us? Now you're being paranoid. We are good people. We go to the chapel every week. We make an honest living out of honest work. Why would God want to punish us?"

"Not all at once," replied Gloria.

"What do you mean?" asked Maria.

"Like I said," Gloria began, "first, about a year ago the fruit and vegetables in the forest rotted away. We can't eat them anymore. Just last night, all our elders died suddenly. And in between all that, a lot of children have been going missing. All these things, are signs." Gloria looked around before focussing on Maria, "Now do you see? This is not a coincidence."

Maria shook her head in disbelief. "How can you be so sure?" she asked.

"Have you heard about Doreen's daughter?"

"No."

"She ran away from home."

"I heard something else," another woman joined in. Gloria almost jumped in fright.

"I think she's been kidnapped. You see, Natalie's son went missing only last week."

"But how can that be? We have not seen any strangers amongst us," said Maria.

"And the five teenage boys," another woman added, "they went camping in the forest a few weeks ago. They said they were going for the weekend but they never came back."

"Where could they go?" Maria asked.

"There is something else that's bothering me too," Gloria added, "I think all the animals are possessed."

"Don't be silly," said Maria.

"Our uncle got kicked by a donkey a few weeks ago. Bruno the butcher's cows broke the fences and escaped. Animals have become really hostile recently. They never used to behave like this," said Gloria. "You know, signs. From God."

"I don't think they have anything to do with each other," said Maria.

Their conversation was interrupted with the sudden scream of a horse. It thrashed about and kicked like a wild animal. It seemed frightened, almost possessed. The owner tried to restrain the horse; he pulled on the reins but he was too weak and powerless. The horse jerked its head from one side to another. The horse screeched. It stomped its front legs onto the owner and kicked its back legs against an unfortunate group of people who stood close by. The horse charged. It ploughed through the crowd injuring everyone in his path and as it galloped away. Members of the crowd came to assist the injured.

"Call the Physician!" someone cried.

Markus and Gretel huddled close to Maria in fear.

Nikolai emerged and rejoined his family.

"What happened?" he asked.

"Some horse went mad and ran away," said Maria.

"It looked really angry, Dad," said Markus.

"It was horrible," moaned Gretel.

"Come on, let's go home." Nikolai lead his family out of the town centre.

***

Nikolai and his family arrived in their little cottage. He sighed with relief.

"What is it?" asked Maria.

"Nothing. It's good to be home after the day we've had," Nikolai replied.

"You still have your axe," Maria commented."Weren't you going to get it sharpened?"

"I'm getting a stone wheel."

"Won't that be expensive?"

"I left a deposit. It'll save me money in the long run. That way, I won't have to pay Shukri to do it for me. He's getting it for me. Anyway, start the fire," said Nikolai.

"Fluffyyyy, where are you? Here kitty," Gretel called out. "Hey Fluffy, come on out, we got some fish."

Suddenly a monstrous creature leapt out from nowhere. With its sharp teeth it bit Gretel on the wrist. It was the family dog. Gretel screamed. The black Labrador growled as it bit deeply into the flesh. It shook its head around to dig its teeth deeper into the wound causing more pain as the teeth met bone. The dog's brown eyes lit up with bloodlust. Its jaw was clamped in place. Saliva dripped from the sides of his mouth. Maria and Markus screamed in helpless fright.

"Rex! What are you doing?!" Nikolai roared. He grabbed the dog and wrestled it to the ground as he reached for the dagger in his belt. The dog barked and thrashed about. And then it turned on Nikolai and attempted to bite his face. It missed.
"Rex... stop it now!" he growled.
The dog still tried to fight him off. With ease, Nikolai slit the dog's throat but the dog didn't whimper in pain. Instead, it tried to fight on while choking on its own blood.

Maria pulled Gretel into a corner and held her in her arms tightly. Gretel cried in pain as Maria looked on in terror. Markus threw himself in front of his mother and sister to shield them from the monstrous dog refusing to die.

Nikolai stabbed the dog through its ribcage. It still tried to resist the pain and fight on. As the blood gushed from his neck, Nikolai held it down.

Each time the dog tried to breath, it only let out more blood from its slit neck. Slowly it lost a small amount of strength at a time, weakened. Nikolai then positioned himself so he can look into one of the dog's eyes. There wasn't one hint of remorse. It was as if the dog never knew his life-long friend. The eyes said it all. "Hate! Die!" The breathing of the dog slowed further and sounded like an old man choking to death.

"Why, Rex? Why?" he whispered.

The dog only tried to growl some more.

Maria and Gretel held each other tightly as they pressed themselves into a corner. They were on their knees while Markus stood in front of them.

Nikolai held his grip on the dog as it became weaker. Its breathing slowed further until finally the dog's cursing eyes closed and his body fell limp.

The family wept, except Nikolai who fought back his tears trying to maintain his stoic appearance.

"Maria, call the Physician." he commanded and Maria got up.
"Come on. Let's cover that up quickly," said Maria. Gretel was still crying in pain.
"Markus, get me a spade," Nikolai said.

***

That night, it was almost dawn when Nikolai felt the arms of his wife wrapped around him and held him tightly as he slept. She pressed her head against his back. She was shivering.
"Hm? Maria?" he mumbled.
"Nikolai," she whispered, "I'm scared."
"What? What is it?" he asked as he rubbed his eyes with his fingers.
"Listen," she said.
"To what?" he asked.
"Shhh! Listen!" she insisted.
Nikolai paused for a moment while his wife latched on to him.

"I can't hear anything," said Nikolai.

"There is nothing," she said, her voice began to tremble. "No birds. There are no singing birds."

"Oh come now," Nikolai tutted.

"Stop it, Nikolai!" she said.

"You're talking nonsense. Birds migrate all the time. They don't stay in one place forever."

"And the owls? What about them?" she pressed.

"So what?"

"I've been listening Nikolai. I have stayed up all night listening. No owls at night. And now, no birds singing in the morning. I don't like this. What's happening, Nikolai?" she asked in sadness.

Nikolai rolled over to face his wife and embraced her.

"Darling, it's only nature."

"Is it? Then what about Mother and Father dying so suddenly, along with the others, all in one night? The rotten food? I heard some people have been sickened by that incense the Priest used at the funeral. The horse that attacked those people in the market. Even our own dog attacked us. What's happening, Nikolai?" she was starting to cry.

"I don't know, Maria. It could be worse. We still have each other." He stroked her hair and kissed her on the forehead. "We have to get on with our lives as normal. Everything in life is a test of strength. We'll be alright. "

***

Dawn broke. Nikolai got out of bed, stretched his arms out, and pushed out his chest. He threw himself onto the floor and did his push-ups. He then went to the kitchen, ate a cucumber, tomatoes, and a boiled egg. All were brought from outside his town. He breathed in the aroma of the food as he chewed. They were tasty, but they were not the same as the ones that grew in the forest nearby. He missed the taste of them. He sighed. Picking up his spare axe, he felt the blade with his thumb, placed it over his shoulder, and then he left the house. He breathed in the morning air. The sky was grey again. It was cloudy, but mild, with the occasional breeze.

Something was missing but he couldn't explain it. Things were not the same as before. There were no birds singing. All the chickens and cockerels had disappeared. As he came closer to the forest, the food he ate earlier left a bad taste in his mouth. Is the food imported from outside affected too? He wondered for a moment. He spat on the ground.

He greeted each and every familiar face he walked pass. Some smiled, some nodded. There wasn't much to say, the pain was still raw. All people could do was carry on with their lives. As did Nikolai. All he wanted was to carry on with his job as a woodcutter and provide for his family like his ancestors did before him. The thought gave him a sense of pride as his walk transitioned into a slight march. He held his chest high and his head up. His long black hair was blowing against the breeze.

He headed towards the forest where the other woodcutters were going. It was always just outside the town as it grew. Despite the countless trees he cut, all the trees looked the same to him. Along the way, he met up with Andreas and Demetri. They greeted each other as they walked.

"How is your daughter?" asked Demetri.
"She's fine. The Physician came, gave her some disinfectant, and wrapped her arm up in a bandage," Nikolai replied.
"Who would have thought it?" said Andreas. "A dog is a man's best friend and all of a sudden it attacks the very family it's supposed to protect."
"Well, things have not been so normal lately," said Demetri. "I heard a rumour that the Mayor plans to get rid of all animals and import everything from outside town. Food, clothing, everything else for all we know. Meanwhile he is putting pressure on us to cut down more trees."
"Hmph. It will cost a lot of money to transport all that. That means he'll raise taxes too," said Nikolai.
"Looks that way," Demetri added. "He's always been greedy. He keeps saying we're not doing our jobs fast enough. Easy for him to say. He can always pick up an axe himself

and help us out."

"Aye," said Andreas, "he doesn't seem to realise that the population of the town keeps growing and there aren't enough woodcutters to keep up with all the demand."

"Huh, more like his demand," said Demetri.

"Not only that," said Nikolai, "but he doesn't seem to want to know how hard our jobs have been getting lately. Have any of you noticed that it's taking more effort to cut down a tree? It's as if the bark of the trees are turning into iron as time goes by. I've had to make more trips to the blacksmith to get my axe sharpened than ever before."

"Yes, I suspected that too," said Demetri, "as a matter of fact I was beginning to think I was getting too old for this job. Heh. But you are right. The barks of the trees are getting harder indeed."

"Perhaps the trees are adapting. Like all living things," said Andreas.

"So be it," said Nikolai, "then we'll have to make better tools. If nature can adapt, so can we."

The three woodcutters reached the edge of the

forest. They sat down on the stumps of the trees they cut earlier to take a break from the walking. They put their axes down.

"Andreas, what are you staring at?" asked Nikolai.
"The forest, it looks different," Andreas replied.
"What are you talking about?"
"I keep a mental record of all the trees that I cut. Just to see where I am. But there is something not right. Look at that tree over there," said Andreas.
"Which one?" asked Demetri.
"They all look the same to me," said Nikolai.
"I could have sworn that tree wasn't there before," said Andreas.

Nikolai laughed, "You've been doing this job for too long. What you need is a holiday."
Demetri joined in with the laughter, "Yes, and with summer coming, the timing is just right to take a long one. You won't need to worry about winter any time soon."
"I'm serious, guys. I don't remember that tree being there," Andreas picked up his axe and

walked towards it.

"Hey! Do you honestly believe that tree came from nowhere?" Demetri asked.

"Let him go. He can start by cutting that one down first. And I'm starting on that one." Nikolai pointed to a random tree.

Andreas approached the tree, he looked up and saw that it looked just as old as all the surrounding trees. He put his hand on the bark, he felt nothing unusual. He let his axe rest on it while he spat in his hands before he rubbed them together. He picked up his axe. He took a hard swing at the tree. As soon as the blade hit the tree, Andreas fell to the ground, as he screamed in agony. He dropped his axe and covered his ears with his hands. His body thrashed about; his legs kicked about in all directions.He looked like he was in immense pain.

"What the hell?!" Nikolai froze as he looked at Andreas, he frowned.

"Good God!" Demetri threw his axe onto the ground and ran over to Andreas who was still thrashing around on the ground, screaming in pain, hands covering his ears and kicking about uncontrollably. Demetri stopped, "Wait. I don't want to touch him. I'll send for help." He ran along the edge of the forest towards the other woodcutters.

Nikolai ran over to Andreas, put down his axe, and tried to hold him down.
"Andreas! Get a grip on yourself! Calm down!" Nikolai put his hands on Andreas' shoulders while he pressed his knee into his abdomen. But it didn't stop Andreas' torment.

Andreas' screams echoed across the edge of the forest and other woodcutters heard.
"Hey! What's going on over there?" one shouted.
"What happened?" another questioned.

Demetri stopped running. He cupped his hands around his mouth and shouted, "Help! Call the Physician!"

***

The Mayor walked over to the Priest's house

accompanied by two armed guards. Behind him, the Physician followed. The Mayor banged on the door. The Priest took a while to answer it. The Mayor walked in as soon as the door opened.

"Pardon the intrusion," said the Mayor. The two guards followed him in, stern, tall, and cold. The Physician entered last.

"What's going on here?" asked the Priest. "You!" he soured his face at the Physician. "What do you want?"

"There is an important matter to discuss," said the Mayor. "That one person at the funeral yesterday, he must have breathed in a lot of the incense fumes. He's terminally ill now. He could die."

"Not true!" bellowed the Priest. He turned to the Physician. "It was you! You poisoned him! To frame me!" The Priest shouted. He coughed.

"Who are you to accuse me of such a thing?" said the Physician. "You seem to be displaying some of the symptoms yourself."

"That's enough," said the Mayor.

"All the other surrounding persons are ill because of it; the symptoms are not so bad. They will be fine," the Physician continued.

"I said that's enough!" the Mayor raised his voice before turning to the Priest. "Somebody is sick as a result of your incompetence. You have no choice but to cooperate. Otherwise I will have you arrested."

"No you won't. The Archbishop won't allow it," he raised his nose up all smug and shook his head.

"Yes, I can. By civil law, I can place you under arrest." The Mayor produced a scroll as swift as though drawing out a sword and pointed at him. The two guards beside him placed their right hands on the hilts of their swords. "There are rumours going around that incense burners are no longer safe. People are asking questions. I want this resolved quickly. It's up to you. Now, provide this gentleman with what he needs. "

The Priest coughed, gagged, wheezed, and then coughed some more. He walked over to a cupboard and looked at a lower section, and froze.

"What's troubling you?" The Physician's words thawed the Priest.

"This can't be right!" He took out a jar, it was full of olive leaves. They were all black as though rotten and burned. He then took out another jar and put it on the table next to the first jar. It also had blackened olive leaves. "The leaves are dried first before I crush them with a mortar and pestle.The leaves and the powder are supposed to be an earthy green colour." He held the two jars next to each other to show everyone. "But they've changed so quickly. How is this possible? One of the jars are newer than the other one. Yet they both looked burnt."

"Where do you get the olive leaves from?" asked the Mayor.
"From the forest. Like always," the Priest answered.
"Looks like we'll have to be importing those too," the Mayor replied. He shook his head.

"Damn it!" he growled to himself. "More importing expenses."

The Physician nodded. "Sir, these leaves are from the same olive trees that we forbade people from eating the olives from. The olives made people sick, remember? Now the leaves are a problem too."

"How is that possible? We've been using the same olive trees for our incense and ceremonies for thousands of years. What could have possibly caused this?"

"I'm not sure yet."
"So what are you going to do?"
"I am going to get some samples from adjacent provinces and compare the results. If I send some messages out today, I should get some responses by next week."
"That is out of the question!" the Mayor barked. "We can't have people from outside interfering with our own affairs. How do you think that will make me look? If the rest of the kingdom hears about this, they will never trust us."

"How will you explain the high demand for imports?" the Physician asked the Mayor.

"Increasing population. Simple. Those woodcutters are going to have to work harder to cut down more trees. The sooner we have more lumber to sell, the better."

"Exactly," the Priest moaned. He coughed again. "There is no need for any intervention. This has already been blown out of proportion."

"Needn't I remind you that someone's life is in danger?" said the Physician.

"I told you. It's got nothing to do with me!" the Priest shouted and then coughed really hard.

"Not until we have evidence to prove that," the Physician declared. "If my theories are correct, I can get you off the hook."

"How dare you all speak to me like a criminal! There is no need for anyone outside our province to get involved," the Priest protested. He coughed again even harder than before, he gagged and then wheezed.

The Physician took out a small vial containing pink liquid from his long coat, "Here's a remedy for that cough." He put it on the table. "One teaspoon in the morning, and one at night. You can thank me later." Then he turned to the Mayor, "Look, I need to get on with this case. I can't do this alone. I need all the help I can get," he reasoned.

"I told you, the answer is no!" The Mayor barked again. "We'll sort this out ourselves. There will be no contact with anyone outside our town without my approval. If you disobey me, I'll have you arrested. Understand?"

The front door swung open.

"Sir," the Physician's apprentice called. He ran up to the Physician panting from the run.

"Somebody needs your help! A woodcutter, he's been screaming in pain since he struck a tree."

"What the - " the Mayor frowned.

"Pardon me, gentlemen. I have to go. Someone else needs my assistance," the Physician left with his apprentice.

***

Nikolai was having dinner with his family. The sun had set, yet noone had seen the sun through the clouds that day.

"Is Andreas alright?" inquired Maria.

"He's fine now. We left him with the Physician," Nikolai replied.

"I went to the market today, and I heard another girl went missing. It's Natalia's daughter this time. She hasn't been seen since last night," said Maria. "I think she's been kidnapped," she added.

"I heard, on the way here. I and the rest of the men have decided to keep an eye out tonight. I'll be standing guard," said Nikolai.

"Will you be doing this every night?" asked Maria.

"Until we catch the culprit," he answered.

There was a moment of silence, except for the cutlery as they ate.

"We have to move," said Maria.

"We're not going anywhere," said Nikolai.

"My job is to cut trees. The town depends on me. If we move out then what will I be doing for a living? How can I provide for my family? We have lived in this village all our lives. Our friends and families are here. Where can we possibly go?"

"I don't like it here anymore Nikolai, I'm

scared," said Maria.

"You have nothing to be afraid of. Things will be fine. I'm here, we have each other. That's all that matters. As long as we carry on as normal we'll be fine."

Nikolai finished his meal and then went to get his axe.

"I'll be standing guard outside," Nikolai explained. "If there is a kidnapper among us, we are going to find him. We're going to find out where all the children have been taken. If there is one thing I'm going to do, is make sure my family is safe. Stay inside."

Along with the other men in his town, Nikolai planted a beacon outside his house. He ignited his torch to light the beacon.

A neighbour walked by with his sword in hand. He looked over to Nikolai.

"Are you ready?" he asked.

Nikolai stood tall. He rested his axe on his shoulder as he held it with one hand, with the other he pointed to the sword and to the dagger attached to his belt.

"All set," he replied with a nod.

The neighbour nodded back."Good.

Are your children safe?"

"Yes," Nikolai replied, "Yours?"

"Safe," the neighbour replied with a nod.

Another beacon was ignited nearby. "Ready!"
another neighbour called out.

"Ready!" one neighbour raised his sword after
he lit his beacon.

Nikolai stood assured. He paced in front of his
house back and forth. After a few marches he
swung his axe, first with one hand, then with
two. He placed his hand on the handle of his
dagger, and then his sword. They were still in
place. Later that night he took out a stool and
sat on it.

Hours passed. The night was silent and slightly
cold. He took in a deep breath and breathed
out. He relaxed for a moment.

"Look alive!" a voice called in the distance.

Nikolai jumped to his feet with his axe in both hands. He was excited for some action. A neighbour within sight pointed to the direction of the forest.

"There!" another called out and pointed to the forest.

"Where?" Nikolai asked. He ran to one direction to get a better view of what's behind the houses. He stopped and froze at what he saw.

There in the distance was a purple mist coming from the forest. Like long arms reaching out to the town it slowly stretched its length. Vast and shapeless, its motion was slow and steady. Like smoke coming out of a chimney on its side, the town breathed in the purple fog. The smoke formed spirals as parts of it twisted and turned, the mist swirled in its slow dance. It was a charming sight. Soon the whole town was immersed in the purple fog, so thick that the beacons became invisible. The fog had a sweet smell. It was so relaxing. It gave off an uplifting mood. It was such a pleasure to be in. One could not keep their eyes open.

***

"Nikolai!" a woman's voiced shrieked.

"Ahhh" Nikolai jumped. "God... what happened?" Before he could comprehend his situation-

"She's gone! Gretel is gone! Our daughter is gone!" Maria screamed.

"No!" Nikolai growled. He picked himself up and ran to his house. There was no one in his bedroom. He looked into the children's bedroom. Only his son was there, rubbing his eyes as he was waking up.

Bewildered, he ran outside. His house was surrounded by neighbours, spreading the news as more of them came to see the unfortunate family. The women cupped their hands over their mouths with shock. The men can only look sympathetically. Nikolai's wife cried.

"Gretel! Gretel! AAAAAAAAAHHHH!" Maria

threw herself to the ground and cried.

Nikolai emerged from the house and stood still. He frowned. He clenched his fists. He gritted his teeth. He could no longer keep up his facade.

NOOOOOOOAAAAAAAAAAAOOOOOOO!!!!

His scream of rage dominated the whole town. Thunder and lightning echoed across the kingdom. The morning rain was awakened, and it poured down heavy rain. The clouds were dark grey. There was no sunshine for this morning.

***

Maria sobbed as she sat next to the Priest in the local chapel.
"There, there, my dear," said the Priest as he held Maria's hands.
"Oh Father, what could we possibly have done to deserve this? Our precious daughter is gone." Maria struggled to hold back tears. She wheezed.

"Don't worry, my dear, she'll be found," the Priest tried to console her.

"When, Father, when? Until then what am I supposed to do?"

"This is all a test, my dear. God works in mysterious ways. I can assure you she will be found. You'll just have to be patient," said the Priest.

"But for how long?" moaned Maria.

"I remember when your mother came to me, wanting to have children, she prayed and remained patient. And then you and your sisters came along. As long as we stay true to our faith, our suffering shall end. All we need is time."

"I hope so, Father. By God, I hope so," sobbed again.

"God is with us," said the Priest, "always was, and always will be."

"Hmph," Nikolai was outside by the doorway of the chapel with his arms crossed. He leaned against the outer wall, and listened in on their conversation. His axe rested beside him against the wall. He looked ahead with a frown carved into his face. "God had no reason to take my daughter," he growled under his breath. He spat on the ground.

"Come on Maria, let's go to my house. Natalia's there too," Gloria put her arm around Maria as she led her away from the Priest. "Here, take this handkerchief."

Maria blew her nose. As they left the chapel, Maria began to cry again. They walked slowly like an elderly couple trying to hold each other steady.

After they left, another woodcutter staggered towards the entrance dragging his feet. In one hand he had an axe, and in the other he held a bottle.

"Harold," Nikolai called out to him. "Are you alright?"

Harold turned to him. He pulled a cynical smirk for a second. "Huh. I will be."

"I heard about your son. I'm sorry," said Nikolai.

"Yeah, I'm sorry too, about your daughter," Harold replied.

Harold looked up at the chapel. His vision

blurred.

"I should have come here more often," Harold began, "all I cared about was my job so I can provide for my family, but I neglected my faith." He sniffed. "Maybe... maybe if I come here every day... you know... to make amends... and then maybe God will forgive me and He'll give me my boy back."

"Don't waste your time," said Nikolai with a cynical tone in his voice, "I've been coming here with my family every week, and now look at me." There was a pause between them. He sighed. "Assuming my daughter is dead, what am I supposed to do for the rest of my life? Am I going to sit around and pray? Ask for forgiveness? For what? I didn't do anything to deserve this. Neither did she."

"You still have your son," said Harold. "My only child is gone. I had a family. And now... what have I got to live for? Huh?"

"We have to keep going. We have to carry on with our own lives," said Nikolai. "We are woodcutters, the town needs us. There are people here who depend on us."

"Yeah, like the Mayor. There's a rumour going around that's he's going to cut our pay and increase taxes," said Harold.

"What? Why?" asked Nikolai.

"I'm not sure. Apparently, it's to cover the import expenses. More like making more profits.

You heard about the woodcutters getting sick from cutting down trees, haven't you? Like what happened to Andreas? Hearing screams and all that. It's slowing down the work force. The Mayor is complaining that there aren't enough woodcutters, and we're not cutting enough wood fast enough. He's ranting and raving everyday over making more money out of wood."

"Yes, and without us he'll be out of work. Without the lumber we cut, this town wouldn't be here. And it's all thanks to the forest. That forest gave us something to do. Work gives us purpose and meaning in life."

"What? Lining the Mayor's pocket? You call that "meaning"? Pah-hah, well I'm going to find something else to do. Maybe this is God's way of telling us to make a career change.

After all, since our taxes pay for the salaries of Priests and Bishops, they live comfortably while we work and strive to get by. So I'm joining the missionary. Starting today." Harold drank the remaining contents of the bottle and threw it over his shoulder. The bottle smashed to pieces on the ground. He belched. "At least my faith and my financial situation will be taken care of. Now excuse me," said Harold. He dragged his feet as he walked into the chapel.

Nikolai remained where he was. He leaned against the wall, arms crossed, while his axe rested beside him still. He sighed.

Just then, Shukri the Blacksmith walked by.
"Nikolai, I just heard. I am very sorry. My family's thoughts and prayers are with you."
"Thank you," said Nikolai. His frown faded; he put his head down.
"Also, your sharpening wheel has arrived. It's in the shop now," said Shukri.
"Thanks, but I can't pay you back right now." Nikolai sighed. "Best keep hold of it until I have enough gold."

"There is no hurry. I know you'll pay the full amount," Shukri replied.

There was a moment of silence until a gust of wind blew between them. The weather was cold and grey. The rest of the town was indoors.

"Come on, Nikolai, let's have a drink. It's on me," said Shukri.
"I don't know," Nikolai replied.
"It will help. Trust me," said Shukri. He walked over to Nikolai and put his hand on his shoulder. Nikolai sighed and picked up his axe. He didn't put it over his shoulder. This time he let his holding arm hang. The blade of the axe was so close to the ground it almost dragged along.

***

Down at the pub, the Physician finished a glass of beer. His apprentice sat beside him. "Sir, I think you should rest," said the young man, "you've been up all night researching as it is."

"I am resting. With my eyes open. It's my brain that needs a little break," he pushed his empty beer glass forward. "Miss! Give me another one!" he called out.

The barmaid nodded. The apprentice sighed.
"Sir, have you heard? Another girl has been kidnapped."
"I know, I am keeping a record of all this. My suspicions are already confirmed. I need you to send this message for me." The Physician handed an envelope containing a letter to his apprentice.
"But sir, you'll get into trouble! And... err... our homing pigeon is dead," said the apprentice.
"I know! Use your head, boy!" he poked the young man's forehead with his finger. "Go with the suppliers, they leave town this afternoon. Say you're a volunteer. They could do with an extra pair of hands. Once you get to the furthest town from here see if you can get someone to send this message for us using one of their pigeons instead."
"But that will take days," said the apprentice.
"I don't care. Just do it!" the Physician commanded. "It's urgent! Get out of here!"

"Yes sir," the apprentice bowed his head. He ran out of the pub with the envelope tucked into his coat.

"Here's your beer," the barmaid placed a full glass of beer in front of the Physician.

He put his hand in his coat pocket, took out some coins and then slammed them on the bar.

"You're welcome," said the barmaid as she took the coins.

Just as the apprentice burst out of the front door of the pub, he bumped into Shukri. The young man's skinny frame bounced off the chubby Blacksmith's belly, the apprentice almost fell backwards.

"Watch it!" Shukri barked.

"Sorry," the apprentice replied. As soon as he saw Nikolai, he took extra care as he walked around him, not wanting to anger the muscular figure before him. He bolted away. The two men entered the pub.

"Shukri! Nikolai!" a familiar voice called.

Demetri was sitting at a table with Andreas on the other side of it.

"Andreas?" Nikolai said with surprise.

"Holy Mother! You're alright!" Shukri exclaimed. "Oh, Miss, two beers please," Shukri barmaid placed his order, "and whatever these two are having."

"Coming up," replied the barmaid.

Shukri and Nikolai joined Andreas and Demetri at the table. Their axes rested beside them.

"Andreas here has been filling me in. It's crazy," Demetri said with excitement.

"How are you feeling?" asked Shukri.

"I'm okay. Still feeling a bit weak though," Andreas replied. "Oh, Nikolai, I heard. I'm sorry."

"Me too," said Demetri.

"Thank you, gents." Nikolai sighed as he placed his axe down to rest next to him. "They've taken my daughter. Now, I fear... for my boy. I think we should barricade our houses at night. You know, too much effort to break in, right? I mean, to get through, they're going to have to make a lot of noise. You know."

"We'll think of something," said Demetri.

The barmaid brought four glasses full of beer. "Here we are, gentlemen," she placed them on the table.

"Put this on my tab," said Shukri. The barmaid walked away.

"Well? What happened to you? Do tell," Shukri urged.

"It's hard to explain," said Andreas. He took a sip of his beer. "All I remember is... I was about to cut down a tree, the next thing... well...." he stopped.

"Yes?" said Shukri.

"I heard a scream. It was constant. It was right inside my ears. It was so loud. It hurt my head," Andreas took another sip of his beer. "But that scream, it scares the hell out of me just by thinking about it. It sounded like a little girl screaming in agony. She must have been in awful pain. Like she was being tortured. The screeching, it just kept going."

"That's all?" Nikolai asked.

"No," said Andreas. This time he took a big gulp from his glass. He swallowed hard before he continued. "There was pain all over my body. It felt like my whole body was on fire....

oh God...as if a thousand needles were being pressed into every bone in my body. And all the flesh around them felt like they were melting. All this faded eventually. But, oh Lord, I'll never forget that."

"I've never heard anything like this before," said Shukri.

"Did you see anything?" asked Nikolai.

"No. It was pitch black. And all screams and pain. That's all I remember," Andreas replied.

"Is it a sickness?" asked Nikolai.

"I don't know," said Andreas, "the Physician won't tell me." He looked over at the Physician sitting at the bar. "He gave me a pain killing remedy that helped me recover. That's it. He won't tell me anything else. Anyway, I'm ready to go back to work. Except..." he paused.

"Except?" Shukri asked.

"I'm worried it's going to happen again. The whole thing lasted hours, but that nightmare felt like it lasted a whole day. And I wasn't the only one. Seven other wood cutters were taken in that day. They experienced the exact same thing I did."

"How?" Shukri asked.

"By hitting a tree with their axes."

"That's crazy," said Nikolai. "A tree can do no harm."

"What? You think I'm faking it?" Andreas replied.

"No. Someone is playing some dirty trick on us." Nikolai growled as he clenched his fist.

"That was no trick! It was real!" Andreas snapped.

"Take it easy, boys," said Shukri.

"You know, I'm beginning to suspect there is something at large here," said Demetri. "Think about it. All our elders died in the same night...um...you know... the way they did.But before that, there was rotten food, kids going missing, animals attacking us, and now this. I mean - pah - woodcutters getting injured from doing their own jobs? This can't be some coincidence."

"There's something else too," Nikolai added, "last night I remember a purple fog coming out of the forest. It was so big. It moved like a tidal wave the way it came at us. Thinking back now, I can only describe it like it was a ghost. A giant ghost!" Nikolai raised his voice.

"Shh! Calm yourself, lad." said Shukri.

The Physician looked over at the four men. Nikolai and the Physician looked at each other for a brief moment before the Physician turned away and gulped his glass of beer down in one go. He got up and made his way over to the four men. He couldn't stand up straight nor walk in a straight line.

"Excuse me, gentlemen, but I couldn't help but overhear your conversation."
"You know something, don't you?" asked Nikolai.
"Perhaps. I have my suspicions. But I'm going to need a little assistance. And maybe..." the Physician paused, "maybe I might be able to help you get your daughter back."
"How?" asked Nikolai.
"Go home, you!" Shukri commanded.
"Ignore him, he's drunk", said Demetri.
"This is not the right time," said Andreas.

"Shut up! I know exactly what I'm talking about. I want to talk to him," the Physician dragged an empty chair along the pub floor, swung it next to the table, and then sat on it.
"Tell me, how?" Nikolai said.

"Oh there is something big going on around here alright," the Physician ranted. "Which is why I requested special assistance from a special someone to help me get to the bottom of this mess. But the problem is, you see, neither the Mayor nor the Priest are going to like it. They would never allow me to get in touch with the likes of this guy. You know, for all the *obvious* reasons. Funny how the Mayor approves of a correspondence between the Priest and the Archbishop and nothing happens. But when I'm trying to do my job, I get told, 'no', 'no', 'no', 'no'. *Bleugh!* Such corruption. It stinks. Why? Because apparently my work is "heresy" or "not legitimate". Hence my predicament."

"So what?" Nikolai replied.

"So I'm going to need a bodyguard. For *him*. And for myself. And in return, I offer you some gold." He dug his hand into his big coat pocket, took out a bag of gold and slammed it on the table. The eyes of the four men widened. Such a huge amount. "You're a hard man. You're exactly what I need. Ready to listen?"

Nikolai looked at the Blacksmith.

"Shukri, the payment for the sharpening wheel is complete."

Nikolai then turned to the Physician.

"I'm listening."

***

A week passed. More children went missing. Nikolai barricaded the front door of his house. He boarded up his windows. He also moved Markus's bed into his own bedroom. Nikolai did his best to stay alert at night while his wife and son slept in the same bedroom. With the help of his new sharpening wheel, he was addicted to sharpening blades. Every night, he sat up holding his axe with both hands. A hand axe was under his pillow, an axe under his bed, another hand axe in the drawer next to his bed, and there was dagger on his belt. There was a row of axes hanging on all four walls. Each one with a freshly sharpened blade.

One day, a black crow flew across the cloudy sky. It headed towards the Physician's house.

It landed on the roof. It cawed twice. The Physician opened his loft window. There was a message attached to the crow's foot. He took it off and the crow flew away. He read the message.

"Excellent," he whispered to himself.

Another week passed.

***

"Come in," said the Physician.

The Mayor and the Priest stepped into the house. The Mayor told two soldiers to wait outside and stand guard.

"This better be good," said the Priest.

"It will be," the Physician replied.

"Well I hope so," said the Mayor.

"Please excuse the mess, I've been experimenting and I have ran out of room in my lab. Would you like anything to drink?" asked the Physician.

"No, nothing for me, thank you," the Mayor replied.

"No thank you," said the Priest.

The Physician lit some lamps in the room.

"Your cough seems to have healed. Looks like that remedy I gave you has worked," said the Physician. The Priest looked away from him.

"Hey, what in the Lord's name are you doing here?" the Priest spotted a big muscular man standing in the corner of the room with an axe over his shoulder.

"I have come for answers," the woodcutter growled.

"This was supposed to be a private meeting -" the Mayor complained.

"Only for us," the woodcutter cut in. The woodcutter ran his thumb along the blade of his axe.

"Gentlemen, please, Nikolai has lost his daughter," the Physician chimed in.

"Nikolai, my son," the Priestswallowed. His hands were trembling. "You have no need to be here. Look, I know you are upset your daughter is missing, but all you can do for the time being is pray."

"Prayers are not enough!" Nikolai slammed his axe onto the table. He let go of the axe to let the handle stick up in the air while he clenched his fists. The Priest jumped in fright and the Mayor shuddered.

"He has every right to be here," said the Physician, "along with all the other woodcutters who have lost their children. Now if you all please sit down,and take your axe off my table."

All the men sat around the table in the middle of the room. Nikolai pulled his axe off the table, and placed it in his lap as he sat. There was one empty chair between the Physician and Nikolai.

"In the name of God, I oppose this. Is all this really necessary?" the Priest complained.

"We need to take action," said the Mayor, "and soon! We cannot afford to lose the money we make from our lumber. There are rumours circulating across the kingdom that our trees are possessed. If we don't undo this mess, we will all lose our livelihoods. Including yours, Priest!"

"But your highness, I have already written to the Bishop. At least let us wait for a response and see what he has to say. Until then, we'll just have to pray."

"There he goes again!" said Nikolai.

"I want results!" said the Mayor. The room fell silent. Then he turned to the Physician, "Well, were you able to find anything?"

"Sir, I have looked at all the cases. Our surrounding wildlife have become hostile. The berries we used to eat are no longer edible. In fact, they have become poisonous. We cannot use the herbs as medicine anymore because they have no effect. The incenses are now toxic. All the town elders were killed off in one night; found cold, stiff, with screaming facial expressions, unnatural causes. The purple mist coming from the forest. Children going missing. The trees have become harder to chop. They are as hard as metal now. Some woodcutters who struck those trees heard screams in their heads and felt like they were on fire. They said they were so loud they became dizzy, they got headaches and then they fainted. It's been getting worse. All this is not some coincidence. I can only conclude this is an act of witchcraft."

"Shhh! Don't say that! You will put a curse on us all!" the old Priest panicked.

"Calm yourself, old man. So what do you suggest we do?" The Mayor remained well composed.

"I know nothing of the dark arts of magic, so I called someone for help."

"What?! You fool! I told you not to message anyone!" the Mayor bellowed. He slammed his fist on the table. Nikolai placed his hand on his axe.

"He is the ONLY person who can help us," the Physician urged. "Nobody else knows about this. He's here right now."

"Why you-!" the Mayor growled. He clenched his fists as he gritted his teeth.

"Do you want this problem solved or not?" the Physician interrupted. "You want to keep this quiet? This is the best way to do it."

Then the Physician turned his head to the cellar door at the back of theroom. "Do come in," he called out.

The cellar door opened. A mysterious figure emerged from the darkness. He was dressed in all black, with a hood. He looked like an assassin. He walked closer to the table. He lifted his hood back with both hands to reveal his face. He was a pale man in his forties with a square jaw, and eye sockets darkened from wrinkles and age. He had seen so much suffering. He stood silent. A pendant hung from his necklace, a silver disc with spiral cut-out.

"Blasphemy?! What is the meaning of this?!" the Priest protested.

"Silence!" shouted the Mayor.

"I don't understand," Nikolai uttered.

"*You... you're a Satanist*! You bring suffering everywhere you go!" shouted the Priest pointing his bony finger at the dark figure.

"On the contrary, your Excellency.It was members of the clergy like yourself who persecuted scholars like these," the Physician defended. "They were hunted and burnt alive. He's one of the few that's left. We're lucky to have him here at all."

"Such insolence cannot be tolerated," the Priest moaned.

"That's enough!" the Mayor shouted again.

The room fell silent. Then he turned to the Occultist."Who are you? What do you do?"

The figure in black sat down on the empty chair next to the Physician. To which the priest turned his chair around so he had his back to the Occultist.He would only see him from the corner of his eye by turning his head, should he ever speak to him. The Occultist ignored him, but the physician sighed as he leaned his face into the palm of his hand.

"My name is Ambrose. I am a scholar of the occult, dark arts, and magic," he paused. "I have looked at all the evidence. I can confirm all this is the work of a Witch," Ambrose said coldly.

"Good God!" Nikolai exclaimed.

"Are you sure?" the Mayor asked.

"I'm certain." The Occultist nodded.

"Can you make spells?" the Mayor asked.

"Yes, but they are not as strong. And they don't last as long," Ambrose replied.

"So what are you going to do?" asked the Mayor.

"Find out what she wants," Ambrose replied.

"Sir I... will you bring my daughter back?"

Nikolai couldn't hold himself back any longer. "No. Witches don't usually return what they take," Ambrose replied.

"Then why are you here?!" Nikolai bellowed. The Priest smirked.

"Young man, needn't I remind you we are mortals who are up against a supernatural being?" the Mayor barked.

"Yes, and he is our only diplomat," said the Physician. "We have to work together. We don't have a choice."

"We are still yet to hear from the Bishop," the Priest was smug in his response. He didn't even turn to look at the other men.

"It will be too late," the Occultist stood up. "I'm starting tonight."

"You just got here. What can you possibly do now?" questioned the Mayor.

"There will be a full moon. The Witch is going to take another child. I must get to work," the Occultist replied.

"Another child?" Nikolai exclaimed, "Who's child is it going to be? How do you know?"

"I feel a disturbing presence. The Witch knows I am here. She will want me follow the child who will bring me to her," Ambrose replied.

He made his way back to the cellar door. "Tell your men to stay indoors. I'm going to follow the child. The Witch will not want anyone else present." He closed the door behind him.

There was a moment of silence until the Physician broke it. "Gentlemen, I think it is time for you to leave."

***

The Occultist got straight to work. Bottles containing different coloured liquids bubbled as he made potions from the ingredients he brought with him. He poured them into small vials and then put them into his cloak. One with purple liquid to make himself immune from the effects of the mist, one with turquoise liquid to keep himself awake and fully alert throughout the night, and a yellow potion to enable him to see in the dark. He made a few extras just in case. Then he placed his sword and his dagger on his belt.

The sun had set. Ambrose stepped outside. He took in a deep breath and relaxed. He pulled the hood of his black cloak over his head. He placed a hand on his spiral pendant and recited a mystical chant to himself. He then placed his hands on his belt, holding his chest high and his head up. He looked on into the direction of the forest.

"Alright," he whispered, "I'm ready."

***

The Occultist walked to the edge of the forest and waited. He stood still. He looked at the trees, scanning each one with his eyes. "Hmm." He felt a certain kind of presence. The inside of the forest was pitch black. He put his hand into the pocket of his cloak, and took out some vials. He drank the yellow potion first. The effects kicked in quickly. As if tiny torches were attached to his eyes, yellow light emitted from them, illuminating everything that was only a few metres from him. He saw everything that was close to him shine yellow with some reddish-orange outlines. It was the perfect map of his surroundings.

Once the moon became full, the Occultist

knew it was time. He looked at the forest and there it was, emerging from the darkness of the forest, the purple fog slowly began to cover the village again. The Occultist next drank the purple potion, the effect kicked in immediately. The purple fog that would put the people to deep sleep vanished from his vision, it had no effect on him. The Occultist saw right through it and knew this was the right moment.

And then he saw a little girl walking towards the forest in the distance. She was a glowing silhouette.Her eyes were wide open;the sockets black but there were no irises, no pupils, just glowing white lights in black sockets. She looked half ghost and half zombie. She slowly turned her head and faced the Occultist, her face had no expression, and she had long black hair that looked wet, partially covering her face. Then she slowly turned away and continued on into the depths of the forest.

First he was intimidated by such a sight, for he had never seen such witchcraft practised on children for he considered them to be innocent and harmless. In his view, whatever the purpose of magic, whatever the forces of evil, they should never include children. Then there was a sense of sadness and pity for the poor girl, and who knows how many other children. Then his sadness was replaced by anger. He gritted his teeth. Such treatment of children. Such injustice of the vulnerable. This should never be allowed.

He followed the girl into the forest. They walked, and walked. It seemed that they had walked for hours as they got deeper and deeper into the forest. As far as he was concerned, he was far behind enemy lines. While meandering through the ancient trees, he took out the vial containing the turquoise liquid. He drank the potion. The potion took effect slowly. He became wide awake, and fully alert. It was enough to keep him going for the rest of the night.

"Is she leading me into a trap?" he thought. But The Occultist knew that he too was just as powerless to the forces of evil and was risking his life. He focused on following the girl, and the girl only.

At last, he saw a faint purple glow in the depths of the forest, and the girl was heading right for it. They walked further and further and the glow of light became brighter. Soon, he and the girl made it; the centre of the forest where no human had ever set foot. The girl stood in the middle of a circle of ancient trees holding light blue lanterns that had a beautiful glow. On the circular ground where the girl stood, was a large spiral carved into the dirt and right in front of the girl was the biggest tree of all that had a wide opening. Inside was not a throne but a bed with purple satin sheets and cushions, and there was a purple glow inside. On this bed lay a beautiful woman, half naked with a thong made of ivy leaves. She had pale skin, long black hair with a purple tint that covered her huge breasts, and she had elegant purple eyes. Her figure was of every man's dream, she was an erotic fantasy personified. She sat up and looked displeased at the sight of a man, for she had a relentless hatred of men.

The Occultist observed. He was puzzled at such a sight for this was nothing he had ever seen before. If this was a Witch, normally they would be ugly old hags, hundreds of years old, but this one was young and beautiful, yet very powerful. What was she doing in the middle of such a forest? What could she possibly want with the children? The Occultist slowly stepped into the circle of trees, took in a deep breath, and spoke; "I have come for the children," said the Occultist.

The Witch stared, she slowly nodded her head, and then out of the shadows around the circle of trees, came the ghosts of all the children surrounding him in a circle. The Occultist was stunned by the number of children she had taken. The children stared at the Occultist with glowing white eyes.

"Why?" he asked.

"These trees are my children, and I am taking them from the people who slaughtered the countless of mine," said the Witch.

"What do you want?" he asked.

"I want you and your people to leave these lands immediately and never come back. I intend to restore my forest exactly the way it was," the Witch replied.

The Occultist then looked at the ghosts surrounding them, but something seemed odd, they were all girls. All the ghosts were girls.

"What have you done with the boys?" he asked.

She gently held her hands in front of her chest, facing each other.They both had black spiral tattoos on her palms. The tattoos began to glow a very bright blue colour which formed an even brighter light between her hands. She conjured a small mirror and sent it floating into the Occultist's hand. The glowing ceased and the Witch placed her hands by her sides and relaxed. As he looked at the mirror, it showed a vision of the boys. All piled up dead at the bottom of a cliff, surrounded by big sharp rocks, reddened by their blood. Their eyes are wide open in fear and their bodies disfigured from their falls and covered in blood.

"NO!" the man shrieked as he dropped the mirror onto the ground.It smashed to pieces and then the pieces melted into the ground and disappeared. The Witch grinned and giggled.

"You can't do this!" he growled angrily. "Leave the children *out* of this!" he stepped towards her.

The Witch glared and narrowed her eyes. Suddenly he felt invisible hands pierce through his skin and grab his internal organs. They were tightened and twisted inside him. He groaned in pain as he collapsed onto the ground clenching his chest with both hands, and his fingers digging into his rib cage. He screamed in pain for a moment. The invisible hands tightened their grip, twisted some more and then they released them and disappeared. As soon as the pain eased off, he took deep breaths and slowly got up recollecting himself. He pulled himself up.

"There's got to be another way," he said.

"You're in no position to bargain with me, mortal. Men like you destroy everything. My patience is gone," said the Witch. Her tone was stern as she spoke slowly. The glare vanished from her face as she looked up.

"There..." she said.

The Occultist looked up and saw groups

of animals in the trees, huddled together, trembling in fear at the sight of the Occultist. "Look how frightened they are," she continued. "Mankind. You did this to them. You are destroying their only home."

"Then why do you choose to terrorise them now?" asked Ambrose.

To that, the Witch conjured a vision of the whole kingdom of Konendara like a floating map hovering above the ground. Like a ghost, it was almost transparent. She zoomed in on the apparition of her forest.
"This is how my forest looked a thousand years ago," she said. The forest was vast. And then the apparition of the forest shrunk to a smaller size. Like worms eating away at a flesh, the edges of the forest vaporised, dozens of trees disappeared. "This is how my forest looked a hundred years ago," she continued. And then even more trees vanished from the edges. The forest looked even smaller in comparison. It was a different shape.
"This is how my forest looks now," she said with a vengeful tone. The forest was even

smaller than before. "Now do you see what they are doing to my forest?" she said. "Now do you understand what I am trying to do?" She paused for a brief moment. "There is no other way."

"The children. What about them? They don't deserve this! Why should the children of these townsfolk be punished for their actions?" Ambrose asserted.

"I am not having them grow up to continue their ancestors' massacre," she said.

The Witch changed the apparition, the forest vanished only to be replaced with visions of woodcutters cutting down trees: one vision after another, axes striking tress, trees falling to the ground like dominoes, one on top of another, animals fleeing in fright, saws cutting the lumber. Like a cacophony of noises, the visions displayed themselves one after another. The sights and the sounds was enough to overwhelm anyone. Then the Witch dismissed the apparition. The ghostly forms of the trees and the woodcutters, and all the barbarity vanished. Then she turned to Ambrose.

"There are too many people eating away at my forest," the Witch continued, "When will it stop? Until there is no tree standing? I am not having that. I am going to restore the balance. I gave them sign after sign but they didn't take heed. I made the vegetation uneatable. I made the animals turn on their tamers, and the rest to seek refuge here. For all the trees they cut down, I took a child, one at a time." She paused for a moment. "I even went as far as to kill off their elderly in the most horrifying manner possible, but even that wasn't enough to deter them. And yet, you, mankind, are such a greedy, stubborn, ignorant race. All you do is consume. My patience is gone."

"What do you want them to do?" asked Ambrose.

"Stop cutting down my trees or leave," said the Witch. "If they refuse, I will destroy them all myself." There was determined sternness in her voice. "You have served your purpose," she paused. "Now, go," she commanded, and then she turned to the possessed girl, still standing in the middle of the circle. "She will lead you out."

The possessed girl nodded and turned to the direction of the town. As the Occultist followed, the Witch began to lay back on her bed, she turned her back to him, and then she fell asleep.

On the way back out of the forest, no twist or turn felt familiar, it was as though the trees shuffled themselves around. No wonder people got lost. All the Occultist could do was obey the Witch for he knew that he was powerless against all supernatural forces. Even if all Occultists came together, they could never resist the powers of real magic. He felt tired from all that experience; he had to push himself more just to get out of the forest. No way he could get out on his own, all he could do was follow the possessed girl. His muscles throbbed in pain, his internal organs ached, and his bones felt heavy. He was sweating, he had a splitting headache as he staggered along behind the girl. The effects of his potions were fading as he grew weaker. At last, the town was visible; it was almost dawn.

The girl stopped at the edge of the forest.

She pressed her heals into the ground, she slowly raised her arms and her long hair began to float. The Occultist saw the girl's feet change into roots digging into the ground, getting bigger and bigger. Her arms and her hair were turning into branches, and leaves began to emerge from them as she grew taller and taller. Her skin went from soft and smooth to a rough tree bark texture. In a few minutes, she looked just like all the other trees.It looked as though the tree had been there for hundreds of years. Then it dawned on the Occultist what was happening to the girls. The Witch would possess the girls and turn them into trees, which explained why the woodcutters heard deafening screams upon striking them. The boys on the other hand would be made to walk off a distant cliff and fall to their deaths. The rest was obvious, her hatred of men, the last thing she needed was for these boys to grow up and continue the dirty work of their elders and desecrate her forest.

The Occultist was exhausted after walking for hours deep into the forest and then back out again, and in between he had his heart, lungs, liver, stomach, kidneys, and other internal organs tightly constricted.They were still hurting. The pain only eased slightly after emerging from the forest. He returned to the Physician's house where he stayed. He wrote a message not to be disturbed and hung it on the cellar door using his dagger. Dawn finally arrived, the sky was grey and cloudy. The effects of all the potions disappeared. His body was racked with exhaustion.He collapsed on to the bed and fell asleep.

***

That morning, Nikolai banged on the door of the Physician's house. He heard the whole town talking about another girl going missing. Members of her family visited the Priest that morning. The Physician opened the door.

"Where is he?" asked Nikolai.

"Not now, son. He needs to rest," the Physician replied.

"The girl."

"I know. I heard."

"What happened to my daughter?"

"I don't know yet. Ambrose is tired. He's

sleeping. He just got back. We're going to have to wait."

"Hmph," Nikolai stormed off.

That afternoon, another group of carts arrived from outside town carrying food and supplies. The Physician's apprentice jumped off one of the carts and walked over to the Physician's house. He walked in. "Sir?" He called out. "Did you hear from him?"

"Yes. He's here. Now hush. He's resting," said the Physician.

The cellar door opened. Ambrose emerged fully recovered. The apprentice froze at such a sight. He had never seen an Occultist before. "Oh hello, Ambrose. Can I get you anything?" asked the Physician.

"No," said Ambrose. "But we need to get the Hell out of here."

***

In the Physician's house, Nikolai, the Mayor, the Priest, the Physician and the Occultist sat around the table again. Once again, two guards stood outside the house.

"Alright, gentlemen," the Occultist began. " Listen to me carefully. You must abandon this town immediately."

"Abandon? That is out of the question! You haven't even told us what happened last night," said the Mayor. "Now tell us the truth."

"I saw her," said Ambrose.

"Don't say it!" yelled the Priest.

"Calm yourself," said the Physician.

"A Witch. The whole time, it was a Witch. She's behind all this," explained Ambrose.

"Good God!" the Mayor exclaimed.

"Unbelievable," Nikolai uttered in disbelief.

"Is there nothing you can do?" asked the Physician.

"No. There is nothing we can do against a supernatural force. She's pure magic. The only thing we can do is obey her command. And that is to leave," Ambrose replied.

"Never!" the Priest protested. "We do not negotiate with evil!"

"Oh yeah? Well, what are you going to do?" asked the Physician. "By the way, has the Bishop written back?"

"That's got nothing to do with you!" the Priest shouted back.

"Silence!" the Mayor yelled as he held his arms up. The room fell silent. He put his arms down. He sighed. He took in a deep breath.

"We don't have a choice," said Ambrose "She has put a curse on this town. The sooner we all leave, we survive." He stood up. "Now excuse me. I have to pack." Ambrose made his way to the cellar door.

"Hold it!" commanded the Mayor. Ambrose stopped in his tracks. "Who else knows you are here?"

"Only us," replied the Physician.

"Now, all of you listen here. Not one word of this leaves this house. You will not tell anyone else anything. No Witch. No Occultist. No curses. Nothing! Understand?"

"You want to keep this a secret? What are you going to do?" asked the Physician.

"You'll leave that to me. It's my job. You've done enough," replied the Mayor.

"If we leave, then how will I do my job?" said the Priest.

"Seek refuge elsewhere. I'm sure there are lots of Churches that require a Priest," Ambrose replied.

"Sir?" Nikolai took in a deep breath. "What

about my daughter?"

"I told you. Witches never return what they take."

"Where is she?" he growled.

"Come with me," said Ambrose.

***

Ambrose and Nikolai walked along the edge of the forest among the stumps. The weather was cold, and dark grey clouds concealed the sun and the sky. Cold wind blew against the two men. Nikolai's long black hair and Ambrose's long black cloak billowed against the wind like flags. Ambrose stopped and so did Nikolai. Ambrose placed his hand on Nikolai's shoulder, and placed his other hand on a tree. He closed his eyes and then opened them.

"Not this one," Ambrose thought to himself as he shook his head. He narrowed his eyes as he looked at the other trees on the edge of the forest. He felt a certain kind of presence among some of the trees. He carried on walking and Nikolai followed.

"What are we doing here?" asked Nikolai.

"All will be revealed," Ambrose replied.

They walked a little further westwards.

"Where is your house?" asked Ambrose.

"Around that way," Nikolai pointed south-west from where they were.

They walked further westwards until they came to a tree that was directly north from Nikolai's house.

"That's my house," Nikolai pointed. It was directly south from where they were.

"Alright, now north from here," said Ambrose. He turned to face north.

There, right in front of him was a tree. It was as tall as all the other trees. Just as old, just as ancient, with bark just as tough. It looked just like all the other trees. They walked up to it. Ambrose put his hand on Nikolai's shoulder and placed his other hand on the tree. Ambrose closed his eyes, took in a deep breath, he opened his eyes.

"Yes. This is it," Ambrose thought. He stepped back. "Alright, Nikolai. I want you to put your hands on this tree. Gently. Close your eyes, and listen."

Nikolai frowned. He stepped forward, stood close to the tree and slowly placed his hands on the tree. He closed his eyes. He listened.

He heard a voice deep inside his ears. A whisper.
"Father."

Nikolai jerked back as he screamed in terror with his eyes wide open. He fell to the ground. His chest went up and down as he panted deeply. He crawled backwards away from the tree for a moment. His eyes were locked on to the tree. Ambrose stood still as he watched. Unmoved.
Nikolai's frantic breathing eased off a little as he recollected himself.
"Gretel?" said Nikolai. He picked himself up and walked up to the tree. He placed his hands on the tree, closed his eyes and listened.

He heard the familiar voice again.
"Father."

Nikolai looked up at the tree.
"Oh my God! What did she do to her?!" he

turned to Ambrose.

"The Witch has turned your daughter into a tree. To punish you in revenge for all trees you cut down. I'm sorry," said Ambrose.

"She turned all the missing girls into trees. And the boys, well, she made them walk off a cliff."

"Oh...God!" Nikolai exclaimed. He wheezed as he could no longer hold back his tears. His chest ached. He could no longer keep up his stoic facade. All he could do was cry as he put his arms around the tree. "Gretel, my daughter," he sobbed.

Ambrose pulled his hood over his head. "You must leave." He walked away.

Nikolai felt weak. He sank to the ground onto his knees while his arms embraced the tree. He began to cry even harder. "Gretel. I'm so sorry." Tears rolled down his cheeks, leaving wet trails down his face that felt cold when the wind blew.

Thunder echoed across the sky. Rain began to

pour down. Still on his knees, Nikolai leaned his face onto the tree as he embraced it. The rainwater ran down the bark of the tree, over his head, and merged with the tears on his face. He closed his eyes, and sniffed. His breathing was unsteady as he cried. He stayed there a little longer.

***

Nikolai returned home drenched from the rain. He took his top off and threw it on the floor. He felt drained. Maria approached him. "Nikolai, where have you been?" she asked.
"I had important business to attend to."
"Which was?" she interrogated.
"Concerning our daughter."
"What?" she gasped. "How? What did you do? Where is she? Oh God, please tell me she's still alive!"
"She is," Nikolai replied.
"Oh thank God," she pressed her hands on her chest. Her breathing became unsteady.
Nikolai paused.
"I don't know how to tell you this, but..." he leaned his back against the wall. He took in

a deep breath as he placed his hands over his face. He removed his hands from his face and looked his wife in her eyes, "Gretel, has been turned into a tree."

"That's absurd! Where did you get that from?" she ranted.

"Because I heard her voice. She spoke to me," said Nikolai.

"What? Our daughter is a talking tree now? Have you heard yourself?" Maria yelled. Nikolai seized her wrist. "What are you doing? Where are you taking me? Let go! You're hurting me."

Nikolai dragged his wife over to the tree where he knelt earlier. He released her wrist. The rain stopped.

"Why did you bring me here?" Maria moaned.

"Here she is," he showed her the tree. "Close your eyes. Put your hands on the tree. Listen."

"Must I?" she stepped forward, and did as instructed by her husband. There was a long silence. Her face looked up at the tree in shock. "Oh my God!" she screamed. "Gretel?! She said 'mother!'...she...she..." she began to weep. "Oh Gretel!" she screamed as though in pain. She closed her eyes. She cried hard. "Gretel.... my ....my baby! My precious little girl." She fell to her knees as she cried. She pressed her chest against the bark of the tree as she expanded her arms in a feeble attempt to wrap her arms around the wide ancient-looking tree. Nikolai sighed. All he could do was watch as his wife cried and wailed at the tree.

"This is my punishment," said Nikolai.

"How!?" she exclaimed.

Nikolai knelt down next to her and placed his hand on the back of her head.

"You see, the Physician hired an Occultist to find out what was happening," Nikolai began. "It was a Witch all along."

Maria gasped. Shocked and confused she shook her head, "H- how could -"

"The Witch has put a curse on us. On me... being a woodcutter."

Nikolai waited for a few moments. The frenzy of Maria's crying faded into silent sobs. Her cheeks were wet from her tears. She kissed the tree and then caressed it. "Gretel," she whispered.

"The Occultist said we should leave this town. But where can we possibly go?" said Nikolai.

"We can't leave her here like this," Maria croaked. Her throat was weakened from all the crying.

"You're right, we can't," Nikolai replied.

With his hand at the back of her head he began to caress her long black hair.

"There is only one thing I can do now. No more cutting down trees," declared Nikolai. "What's done is done. There's no reason for the Witch to punish us any further. There's no need for us to go anywhere."

"But what about the other woodcutters?" asked Maria. "What will they do?"

"What the Witch said was clear. She doesn't want us cutting down trees. Besides,if they carry on, they suffer the same fate as us. They have to find work elsewhere," said Nikolai.

"And you? What will you be doing?" she asked.

"I already thought about it. Now that I have my stone wheel, I can sharpen blades for a living," Nikolai replied. "Come on. Let's go home." He lifted her to her feet and then put his arm around her. Maria put her arms around her husband, she leaned on him as they walked.

As they walked home, they stopped, they both turned to face the tree behind them, then they looked into each other's eyes. They had an idea. Nikolai took out the pickets of the fence around his house and put them in a wheelbarrow. He picked up a mallet and a spade, and then put them in. Maria weaved a long scarf and took out some ribbons. Then Nikolai and Maria went back to the tree, they placed their hands on the tree to make sure it was Gretel. Then Nikolai took out one picket at a time and hammered it into the ground with his mallet. One by one he formed a large circle of pickets around the tree. Maria tied the pickets to one another with the long scarf she weaved. Then she tied ribbons onto the scarf in between the pickets. The whole thing looked like an ancient shrine. Once they finished, Nikolai and Maria stepped back. Maria recited a prayer. They took one last look and went home.

***

The next morning, the bells of the town centre's cathedral rang. The weather was cold, the sky was grey and cloudy again. The bells echoed across the town as the townsfolk made their way to the town centre.

The Priest stood on a pedestal. He was surrounded by a group of the Mayor's armed guards. Behind the Priest was the Mayor who was also surrounded by a group of armed guards. The Priest held a scroll in his hand.
The Physician's house was on the other side of the town centre. The Physician and his apprentice opened the windows and leaned out. Some people in the crowd were talking among themselves.

"Children of God," the Priest began, "lend me your ears." The crowd fell silent. "I have received a letter from the Archbishop himself," he showed off the scroll. "As I have expressed your grievances to him, he has given me the answer. From missing children to rotting food, this is all a punishment from God. We now know who is responsible for all this. He is living among us."

The crowd gasped as they looked at one

another in dismay.

"For years he has plagued our community with blasphemy and heresy. He constantly challenged the validity of the church, which is akin to questioning God himself."

"Who is it?!" some members of the crowd yelled.

The Priest pointed to the Physician's house.
"It's him! The Physician! Hiding behind his so-called knowledge of science. It is no wonder he never goes to the chapel. His lack of faith has put a curse on us all."

The crowd turned to face the Physician with scorn.
"That's not true!" yelled the Physician.
"The Physician has brought this curse upon us," the Priest continued.
"I have lived in this town all my life! I never brought a curse upon anyone!" the Physician shouted.
"He works for the Devil!" shouted the Priest.
"Priest, what are you trying to do?!" shouted

the Physician. "It's not me!" he yelled. "There's a Witch in the forest. It's the Witch's curse. She told us to leave this town." "Mayor!" the Physician called out to him. "I thought you said you wanted to keep this quiet."

"What? The Mayor knew?!" a member of the crowd said.

"Lies! Lies! All of it!" the Mayor shouted at the top his lungs.

"Well since you brought this curse upon us. Why should we believe you?" someone called out.

"Listen to me," the Physician yelled at the crowd. "Was it not I who cured you of your illnesses? Was it not I who found remedies to sicknesses across the kingdom? It is my job to do scientific research. It is my job find things out. Mark my words, everything you've seen is all supernatural."

"How do you know?" someone asked.

"We hired an Occultist to investigate the matter, he-"

"We?! It was you! You brought him here! You're the one who made this plague worse," shouted the Priest.

"The Occultist told us about the Witch. The Witch told us to leave! We must leave! It's too late. There is nothing else anyone can do," said the Physician.

"But what if the Physician is right? What if there is a Witch?" another member of the crowd called out to the Priest.
"There is no Witch!" the Priest dismissed.
"You liar! You were present when the Occultist told us it was the Witch. Why do you deny it now?" yelled the Physician.

Everyone in the crowd looked at one another. They asked each other questions. There was mass confusion.
"The Priest knew?"
"Why would a Priest have any dealings with the occult?"
"That doesn't make any sense."
"Where's the Occultist now? Why won't he tell us?
"Why would the Physician make this up?"
"What did he mean the Mayor wanted to keep it quiet?"

But then a woman shrieked "The children!" It was followed by an uneasy silence. "What about the children?! What have you done to them?" she screeched.

"The Witch took them!" the Physician answered. "She has immense powers."

"There is no Witch!" the Mayor stepped forward. "They were kidnapped. We don't know by whom. But we know one thing, as the Priest here is my witness, the curse has been brought upon us as punishment by God. And so we have come to the decision to expel the Physician from our town."

"Yes! Exile!" someone from the crowd shouted. "Expel him!" Another voice agreed.

"No! Wait! You can't expel me! I'm innocent!" shouted the Physician.

The Mayor stepped forward, stood in front of the Priest, and pointed at the Physician. "As Mayor of this town, it is my duty to ensure the wellbeing of my people. I hereby order this Physician to leave. Immediately! Everyone, throw him out!"

The crowd was aroused with mutual anger. All the men and women ran towards the Physician's house and broke down his front door. Within a minute the Physician and his apprentice were dragged out of the house. Some members of the crowd threw eggs and tomatoes at them. The rest threw punches and kicks along with slaps while others spat on them.

"Get out! Get out!" the crowd shouted. "Don't ever come back!"

As soon as the Physician got on to his feet he ran for his life. His apprentice followed. They ran until they disappeared from sight.

The angry mob then grabbed all the Physician's belongings, brought them out on the street, and threw them on the floor. Scrolls, maps, potions, glasses and beakers, globes and models, and diagrams; everything the Physician owned was out on the ground. Destroyed.

At this, the Priest and the Mayor looked at

each other and smirked. They walked into the Cathedral. Their armed guards followed. They slammed the doors shut.

***

Later that day, Nikolai went over to Harold's house. He knocked on the door, Harold answered it.

"Nikolai?"

"I need to talk to you," said Nikolai.

"Oh aye, do come in."

Harold was dressed in a new white robe with gold patterns on it. It was a Priest's uniform.

"I would offer you a drink but I have none," said Harold. "I gave it all up."

"So you really have joined the missionary," said Nikolai.

"Yes, I have not been assigned to a church yet," said Harold. "So what is it you want to speak to me about?"

"I heard about this morning. The Physician has been exiled. Why?" Nikolai enquired.

"Yes, not the most pleasant way to start the day. The Mayor and the Priest had him exiled for bringing the curse upon the town. So he was thrown out."

"But... what about the... what did the Priest tell you? About the Physician?" Nikolai asked, confused.

"Nothing. Nothing at all."

"He didn't tell you about a meeting?" asked Nikolai.

"No. But with whom?"

"Look. The night before, we had a meeting," Nikolai started. "There was him, the Mayor, the Priest, and I. But there was someone else too. An Occultist. He was hired to investigate our problems. And he told us that it was a Witch. He saw her. She is punishing us."

"The Priest never mentioned any of that to me," said Harold. "But this Occultist fellow, what else did he tell you?"

"The Witch took our children. To punish woodcutters. For cutting down her trees," said Nikolai.

"Her trees? Since when did the forest belong to anyone?" asked Harold.

"That's not the point. She has powers. She was the one who killed our elders. She was the one who made all our food rot. She was the one who made animals go mad and flee. Now do you understand? It was her all along. And I'm telling you, she took our children."

"So where are they?"

"I'm sorry Harold. Your son is dead," said Nikolai.

"How do you know?" asked Harold.

"The Occultist told me. The Witch, she made them walk off a cliff," Nikolai replied.

"Oh aye, then where is your daughter?" asked Harold.

"She got turned into a tree," Nikolai answered.

"PAH-hahahaha! You damn fool. Am I supposed to believe that? Get out." said Harold.

"Listen to me Harold, it's Gretel, she spoke to me."

"Aye, talking trees," Harold mocked.

"Come and see for yourself," Nikolai urged.

"I said get out!" Harrold barked.

"Fine. Don't say I didn't try to tell you." Nikolai stormed out.

***

The next day was cold and grey. The sky was cloudy. That morning, there was a knock on the front door. Nikolai answered it.

"Hello Gloria," he said.

"Hello Nikolai, is my sister in?" she asked.

"Here I am," Maria approached.

"Maria, we're leaving now. I've come to say goodbye." Maria and Gloria embraced.

"Are you packed up as well?" asked Gloria.

"No. We've decided to stay," Maria replied. She held Nikolai's arm.

"What? Why?" Gloria exclaimed.

"It's complicated." Nikolai joined in.

"Did you see anyone else?" asked Maria.

"Yes. I saw Andreas and Demetri going to work."

"What?" Nikolai gasped.

"Well of course," said Gloria, "the woodcutters are collecting one last batch to take with them before they leave."

"No!" Nikolai gasped. He ran to the bedroom, seized a newly sharpened axe and ran out of the house. With haste he ran as fast as he could.

"No! No! No! Have they gone mad?!" he growled to himself as he ran. "Don't you people learn?"

He reached the edge of the forest where he saw hundreds of woodcutters cutting down the trees. But something seemed odd about them. None of them were familiar faces. They were all strangers for he had never seen them before. He stopped. He threw his axe onto the ground. Cupped his hands around his mouth and shouted as loud as he could.

"HEY! What are you doing?! Stop! Stop it now! The Witch!" he paused to get his breath back. All the woodcutters who heard looked at Nikolai puzzled.

"What are you talking about?" one woodcutter said.

"We came from other parts of the kingdom," another woodcutter said.

"We were hired by the Mayor," said another.

"What! Why?" Nikolai exclaimed.

"Apparently there isn't enough lumber to keep up with the demand," answered another woodcutter.

"Don't you understand?!" Nikolai bellowed. "This is why we're cursed! Stop cutting!"

Suddenly, he heard a scream. He turned around. It sounded like someone familiar. "Gretel? No!" He picked up his axe and ran towards the tree that Gretel was turned into. He reached it. There was a woodcutter on the ground. He had picked off three of the pickets from the ground to get to it. This woodcutter was also a stranger. He screamed in pain as he kicked about while his hands covered his ears. Next to him on the ground was his axe.

"You fool!" Nikolai barked. "Can't you see there's a fence around it!" He helped him up. He threw him over his shoulder. He held the man with one arm while he carried his axe in his empty hand. He carried him to the town centre.

Nikolai carried the woodcutter until they reached the town centre, but it was empty. There was no one in sight.
"Somebody help!" Nikolai called out. "We need medical assistance! Now!"
There was no response from anyone.
"Damn!" said Nikolai annoyed. He knelt down and put the weakened woodcutter on the

ground. "Don't worry. Just rest. Okay?"

Suddenly, there were screams coming from every direction in the town. The screams were so loud and high pitched, it made Nikolai tremble for a moment. "What the hell is going on?" He picked up his axe, stood up, and looked around.

Just then, a man ran out of his house while his wife chased after him. She screamed. She lunged at him and tried to claw his eyes out with her fingernails.

Another man stumbled out of the front of his house covered in blood. His wife and teenage daughter ran out of the house and also screamed loudly throughout. They had knives in their hands and they stabbed him to death. He was already on the floor when they raised their knives and plunged them into the corpse. The woman and the girl jumped up and looked around. They spotted Nikolai. They emitted a high-pitched scream as they jolted into a run towards him. Their speed was immense.

Their eyes and mouths were wide open. The irises of their eyes glowed yellow, while the sclera of were black. Their eye sockets were black. They looked like possessed demons. They raised their knives in the air as they ran towards Nikolai screaming at the top of their lungs.

They had long pointed fingernails and long pointed teeth.

"Oh my God!" Nikolai froze in fright for a moment before he came to his senses. He held his axe with both hands. He planted both feet firmly on the ground. He raised his axe and twisted his upper body to the right. He stood still while he waited for them to come closer. Closer. Closer. Closer.

Then he took a swing at the mother's head. It silenced her. The teenage daughter jumped forward with her left arm stretched out and her right hand that held the knife raised. She tried to grab Nikolai's arm but he pulled away just in time. But her claws scratched his wrist. He smacked the possessed woman with the back of his left fist. He knocked her off balance. In that moment he raised his axe in the air and held it with both hands, and chopped the woman in half from top to bottom.

Nikolai tried to catch his breath. All those loud screams from the possessed women gave him a headache. But more screams filled the air as they echoed across the town.

"Nikolai!" a familiar voice called.

Shukri emerged from his shop with a hammer in his hand. The hammer and his right hand was drenched in blood. He breathed heavily to get his breath back. There was tears in his eyes. "My wife," he moaned. "She tried to kill me! I... I had to...God damn it I had to do it." He extended his arm to show Nikolai his blood-soaked hammer. "She turned into a monster. She tried to kill me."

"Shukri! What's going on?!"

"The women," said Shurki. "They've gone mad. They are attacking men like wild animals. They've turned into banshees! They won't stop screaming!"

Nikolai and Shukri looked around as they witnessed the horror their town was in. One man had a banshee's hands tied up.He dragged her along the ground by the hair as she screamed, and threw her into a well. In the distance, another man ran out of his house while a banshee threw things at him, and then she lunged forward, grabbed him by the neck and strangled him to death.

"My God!" Shukri exclaimed. Then he turned to Nikolai."Nikolai! Where's your wife?"

"She's at home. With my son - oh no!" he gasped. He ran to his house.

***

Nikolai ran as fast as he could. His chest hurt from running with such haste and panic. He reached his house. The front door was open. But it was quiet. There were no screams. He ran inside. All the furniture was overturned.

And right in front of him was the mutilated corpse of his son in a big puddle of blood. His blue eyes were wide open as they stared at the ceiling. His mouth was open with shock. Right next to him was his mother, eating away at his flesh. She devoured his abdomen, slurped and sucked as she chewed on his intestines. In her hands she had knives which she had plunged into him. One into his chest, the other in his groin. The fists firmly held the knives as they locked the boy in place while she ate him.

Suddenly, with lightning speed, she raised her head, and emitted a high-pitched ear-piercing scream at Nikolai. She jolted up to her feet and attacked him. Her eyes were all black with glowing yellow irises.Her mouth was wide open with long sharp pointed teeth. She had the face of an old hag. The knives in her hands were raised high as she attempted to slash at Nikolai.

Nikolai jumped backwards in fright. "NAAAOOO!" He cried as he ran into the bedroom. He seized the hand axe from under his pillow with his right hand. For his left hand he pulled the dagger out from his belt. The screaming banshee chased after him. She jumped forward with both knives held forward. Nikolai moved out of the way but she slashed him at his shoulder and back. Nikolai growled in pain. He took a swing at her face with the hand axe. Her scream continued to dominate the house. He screamed. "Diiiiiieeeee!" He plunged the dagger into her neck. He held it in place as he chopped at her back and forth with his hand axe. His right hand was a rapid sawing machine as he chopped like a madman at the banshee. Every chop was another burst of blood that splashed around the room. All over the walls, all over the ceiling, all over the bed and the furniture. With the banshee weakened, Nikolai pulled the dagger out of her neck and threw it away. The hand axe, he threw down. He grabbed an axe hanging on the wall, held it in both hands, spun his torso to the right and swung his axe to the left, and sliced her head off. The blade was so sharp it passed through the neck like cutting a small thin branch. It wasn't enough. "Diiiiiiieeeeee!" he screamed again as he pulled the axe back in position and took another swing at her. He chopped her body in half. He threw the axe away. Seized another dagger from his belt and stabbed the banshee again and again. He plunged the dagger into the body of the banshee until his frantic anger subsided. He was out of breath. He panted. He rasped as he pushed himself away and threw himself on the floor. His chest went up and down rapidly as he regained the rhythm of his breathing. His face, his long black hair, his hands, and his body were soaked in blood.

Nikolai turned over, picked himself up, and stumbled as he made his way to the room where his dead son lay. He fell to his knees next to his son. He closed the boy's eyelids. His hands trembled as he held his son in his arms. He rocked backwards and forwards. He began to cry.

"Why?" he moaned. "Why?" he wailed as tears rolled down his cheeks. He held his son a little longer before carefully laying him back on the floor gently. He stood up and looked down at him. His senses were reawakened when he heard screams echo across the town.

Like a drunk man he stumbled outside to the front of his house. He saw some corpses scattered by the streets, and smoke from houses that were on fire.

He closed his eyes tightly. He gritted his teeth. He shook his head. He looked up at the grey clouds that filled the sky. He growled with all his might, and all the air in his lungs, he exploded.

AAAAAAAAAAAAAAAAA HHHHHHH !!!!!!

He growled, "I'm gonna kill her!" He ran back into his house. "I'm gonna kill that Witch!!!" He had an angry frown permanently chiselled into his face. Nikolai grabbed the two daggers and placed them into their sheaths attached to his belt. He picked up the hand axe and put it in his belt. He grabbed a newly sharpened axe from the walls. He had one big axe for each hand. He growled as he breathed. He was ready.

"Nikolai!" familiar voices called from outside. "Are you there?"

Nikolai stepped out of his house. Demetri and

Andreas stood with their axes in their hands. Their eyes were red from weeping.

"Oh my God," said Andreas.
"You too," said Demetri.

"What?" said Nikolai.
"Our sons. They got our sons," Demetri moaned.
"I'm gonna kill her," said Nikolai.
"We all are," said Andreas. "We're gathering at the town centre. Outside the cathedral. Right now."

***

In the town centre, there was an angry mob. The cathedral was on fire. The windows were smashed. The roof crumbled down as the tiles rained down to the ground. The exterior stone masonry remained standing while everything else inside collapsed. Outside the front door of the cathedral stood two flagpoles, but the flags bearing the town's heraldry were removed. Instead, on top of each flagpole was an impaled head. One held the head of the

Mayor, the other held the head of the Priest.

It was late afternoon and the screams of the banshees were gone. All that was left of the town were men. Farmers with pitchforks and sickles. Butchers with sharp knives and meat cleavers. Woodcutters with axes. Blacksmiths with hammers. The town soldiers had swords. The rest held torches.

Right in the middle of the town centre was Shukri the Blacksmith. He stood with a gigantic hammer in his hands. They all had one thought, "KILL HER!"

Nikolai, Demetri and Andreas joined in with the crowd. Shukri noticed them.

"Are we all here?" Shukri shouted.
"Aye!" all the men shouted as they raised their weapons into the air.
"Are you ready?!" Shukri shouted.
"Aye!" the men shouted again.

Shukri pointed his hammer to the direction of the forest. At the top of his voice, he shouted:

"GET HER!"

The angry army of men charged towards the forest. They screamed with rage as they ran. The ground shook by their ferocious stampede. Shukri ran waving his hammer around over his head. Nikolai screamed with rage with his mouth wide open. The fire in his stomach raged with excitement. As fast as his legs could carry him, he ran like never before. Sharps axes in his hands. Ready to fight to the death.

They all ran into the forest. They ran as fast they could. Some hacked branches as they passed. They screamed with rage. Each one had a slogan of his own.
"Kill the Witch!"
"Kill that bitch!"
"Die!"
"Burn in Hell!"
All merged as one scream of vengeance.

The clouds above turned a very dark grey, and then a violent thunderstorm began. Thunder and lightning echoed across the sky.

A hailstorm commenced, hailstones as big as fists pounded the men in the forest as they ran. Each one felt as though someone threw giant stones at them. Some dented their skulls and killed them straight away. But this did not deter the men's angry charge. They screamed again with rage.

Out of nowhere, they heard a strange noise coming from deep within the forest. It rapidly got louder and louder. A colossal of black clouds appeared.It sounded like it was buzzing, the cloud soon dominated the sky blackening it. The cloud finally descended upon the remaining population at an extraordinary speed. The cloud was made of millions of bees, wasps, mosquitoes, flies, bats and crows. These creatures were larger than normal. The bees and wasps flew right at the men with their stings ready in position as they plunged into the skins of all the men like giant darts. They poisoned the men with toxic stings that felt like burning hot nails being pressed into their skin. Each man suffered a hundred of these stings. Bats and mosquitoes latched onto them, bit them, and sucked their blood.

Flies flew onto the men and ate away at their wounds. Crows pecked and scratched with their claws, all of them tearing away small pieces of flesh at a time. All the men screamed in agony throughout this supernatural assault on them. They were eaten alive.

Within a short period of time, there was nobody left, only bones remained. The empty town was in ruins. As quickly as the cloud of insects arrived, they returned deep into the forest. The sky was still covered with dark grey clouds and then a thunderstorm began one last time, it started to rain heavily. The rain became heavier and heavier. It was raining so hard; it was hard to see through it. It was as if the clouds released waterfalls from above.

As the heavy rain continued to fall, the earth started to shake and the land began to change. Millions of giant invisible ploughs turned the ground over. The soil twisted and turned inside out as the ground caved in on itself, wet and pure like the earth was reborn. Thousands of trees burst out of the ground. Upon each explosion in the soil, a new tree thrust itself out and expanded its branches. Thousands of leaves burst from each branch. The forest began to seize the lands of its original empire and flourish once more. The trees shot up from the ground and grew at an immense speed. The territory of the forest grew and grew. It was a relentlessly unstoppable force. It reclaimed every stump and made it into a new tree. The heavy rain was a perfect cover to conceal all of this. It rained heavily for days and nights, and as it did, more trees grew out of the ground at fast paces and appeared to look hundreds of years old. Each one, fresh and strong. When the rain stopped, the grey clouds retreated elsewhere. The sky was finally blue and clear. There was only brightness.

At last, when the sun shone on the forest, it was in its purest form. The family of trees were fresh and strong. All plant life, all vegetation;lush, moist and pure.

The bushes were decorated with colourful flowers, each one giving off their sweet scents. Bees buzzed around them as they collect their pollen to make delicious honey. Plants with sweet tasting berries and spicy herbs grew. The animals lived with joy and bliss in their beloved habitat. Birds of all shapes and sizes sang their songs as they built their nests. Owls slept inside trees snug, as they waited for sunset. Squirrels leapt from branch to branch as they chased each other, their mating season had begun. Badgers, moles, and rabbits emerged from the ground. Deer feasted on the new and succulent grass. Butterflies danced in mid-air as they flapped their splendid wings. New rivers passed through with clean water, clear as crystals, filled with fish. Ducks swam on the surface of the water with their ducklings.

The forest was once again back the way it was, so natural, so pure, so beautiful. It was as if there were never any settlers. As if no tree, not even a leaf was ever touched by mankind.

The End

Mustafa Kulle

is an Office Manager in a recruitment firm who worked as a freelance graphic designer, and as an IT Technician since he graduated in Hertfordshire University in 2008. In his spare time he reads, sings rock songs, writes stories, and he can draw anything. His imagination is a whole universe of its own. With a passion for everything to do with Japan, he loves Japanese history, the cuisine, movies, video games, and he has a Black belt in Karate. He enjoys heavy metal. He lives in Southgate, London.

www.MustafaKulle.com

Follow him on Instagram:
Mustafa Kulle aka @MusgravePanther

Other titles from the Author:

Just Business...

School Shooter

Trevor